RUBBLE TO THE RESCUE

Bath · New York · Cologne · Melbourne · Delhi
Hong Kong · Shenzhen · Singapore

This edition published by Parragon Books Ltd in 2016

Parragon Books Ltd
Chartist House
15–17 Trim Street
Bath BA1 1HA, UK
www.parragon.com

By Kristen Depken
Illustrated by MJ Illustrations

ISBN 978-1-4748-5703-1

Printed in China

This book belongs to

_____

_____

The PAW Patrol pups loved to watch their favourite hero, Apollo the Super Pup, save the day in his own super way.

"Wow!" Rubble said when the show ended. "Isn't Apollo the super-est Super Pup ever?"

Just then, Ryder walked in and invited the pups to play football outside. "Coming, Rubble?" asked Ryder. "No thanks," said the pup. "I'm going to play Rubble the Super Pup and save the day my own way."

"Hmm ... who can I save?"
Rubble asked Ryder.

"Farmer Yumi might need
some help around the farm,"
he suggested.

"Great idea, Ryder," shouted
Rubble, as he headed straight
out the door.

"Hi, Farmer Yumi," Rubble called as he arrived at the farm. "Need a Super Pup to save the day?"

"My chickens flew the coop when I left the door open," she explained. "Can you help, Super Pup?"

Rubble ran at a group of chickens, and they leaped into the air in surprise. Then he steered the startled chickens back into their coop.

"Is there anything else Rubble the Super Pup can do for you?" he asked Farmer Yumi.

"Mayor Goodway might need some help," she replied.

"Rubble the Super Pup is here to save the day!"
Rubble said as he arrived at City Hall.
Mayor Goodway dashed past him looking worried.
"Hi, Mayor Goodway," Rubble called.

"You're just the pup I need," she said. "There's been a rockslide and the train is stuck inside Mountain Tunnel."

"Don't worry, Mayor Goodway," Rubble said. "Rubble the Super Pup is here to save the day!"

Rubble decided he didn't need to stop Ryder and the pups' football game – he could save the day his own way!

"I knew the PAW Patrol would save the day!"
said the train engineer when Rubble arrived at
the tunnel. "But where is Ryder and the other pups?"
   "Rubble the Super Pup can handle this!" said Rubble.
"Just like Apollo the Super Pup does – all on my own!"

The engineer wasn't so sure. He was worried that more rocks could fall down if Rubble wasn't careful. But the Super Pup was confident that he could save the day.

Rubble charged at the fallen rocks, but they wouldn't budge. He charged again, this time pushing a boulder out from underneath the rockslide.

"Look out!" shouted the engineer as more rocks fell down, blocking the entrance completely.

"Quick! We have to get out the other side," said Rubble.

But as they raced towards the other end of the tunnel, more rocks fell down and blocked the exit.
"I'm sorry," Rubble said, sinking to the floor.
"I thought I could do it myself, but I've just made everything worse."

Rubble sat up. He knew exactly what to do: yelp for help! The tag around Rubble's neck lit up as he called Ryder and the PAW Patrol.

"Hi, Ryder," said Rubble. "I need the PAW Patrol here on the double! There was a rockslide at Mountain Tunnel and now we're trapped!"

"Don't worry, Rubble," Ryder said. "No job is too big, no pup is too small! We're on our way."

Using his PupPad, Ryder gathered the rest of the PAW Patrol and set off to rescue Rubble. The PAW Patrol was on a roll!

The PAW Patrol arrived at
Mountain Tunnel, ready for action.
"Chase is on the case!" Chase said.

He used the winch on his police truck to move some of the rocks and create an exit.

Rubble squeezed through the gap. "Thanks, Chase," he said. "Now, how can I help?"

Moments later, Rubble jumped in his digger.

"Okay, Rubble," said Ryder, giving Rubble
a big thumbs up. "You know what to do."

Rubble drove his digger towards the rockslide.
He scooped up the rocks blocking the tunnel and
moved them safely away.

When all the rocks had been moved, the engineer drove the train out of the tunnel. "Rubble, you did it!" he cheered. "You saved the day – your own way!"

Rubble shook his head and smiled at Chase and Zuma. "You mean I *helped* save the day – the *PAW Patrol* way."

As the train pulled away, the engineer tooted the horn in thanks. Ryder gave each of the pups a pat on the head to congratulate them on saving the day.

"Now let's go and play together," said Rubble. "The PAW Patrol way!"